THIS BOOK BELONGS TO:

Made in United States
Orlando, FL
17 September 2023

37018779R00061